JACK

THE HAUNTED LIGHTHOUSE

ZANDER BINGHAM

GREEN RHINO
MEDIA

www.greenrhinomedia.com

First Printing: September 2018

Green Rhino Media LLC
228 Park Ave S #15958
New York, NY 10003-1502
United States of America

www.jackjonesclub.com

ISBN 978-1-949247-01-5 *(Paperback - US)*

ISBN 978-1-949247-04-6 *(Paperback - UK)*
ISBN 978-1-949247-07-7 *(eBook – US)*
ISBN 978-1-949247-10-7 *(eBook - UK)*

Library of Congress Control Number: 2018954294

DEDICATION

This book is dedicated to my two
adventurous sons, Xavier and Greyson.
May your minds always be open.
Never stop learning and be forever curious.
Explore everywhere and
everything you can.

CONTENTS

DEDICATION...iii

ACKNOWLEDGMENTS vi

CHAPTER ONE...1

CHAPTER TWO 11

CHAPTER THREE 23

CHAPTER FOUR 35

CHAPTER FIVE 45

CHAPTER SIX...55

CHAPTER SEVEN.. 66

CHAPTER EIGHT 79

TITLES IN THIS SERIES 92

ABOUT THE AUTHOR............................... 93

ACKNOWLEDGMENTS

To my incredible wife, Diana, you are amazing. Thank-you for your help in bringing Jack Jones to life.

To my eldest son, Xavier, I could not have asked for a better audience to listen to the countless drafts of Jack's adventures. Your ideas, questions and input were invaluable.

To Kris, Allan, Felix and Gina, without your encouragement and support, this journey would simply not have been possible.

To Andrea, your illustrations brought us into Jack's world and enabled us to fully engage in the story and connect with the characters.

To Claire, your time and devotion, constructive feedback, attention to detail and real-world factoids helped maintain believability in an otherwise made-up story.

To friends and family members who have stuck by me in this new writing venture, please enjoy what your support has helped create.

CHAPTER ONE

It was late-morning on a spectacular, early Spring day. Mr. and Mrs. Jones, along with Jack, Emma and Albert in the backseat, pulled off the main road and began down the long driveway toward the coast.

A light dust blew up behind the car and the sound of gravel crunching beneath the tires was a welcome change for everyone, after several hours of driving, a ferry ride and countless games of *I Spy*.

Emma was the first to see it and called out excitedly, "There it is! I can't believe we get to stay in a *real* lighthouse!"

The distinctive red-striped tower of the lighthouse rose quickly from the horizon of brush and sand dunes as they approached.

Mr. Jones looked at Emma in the rear-view mirror as he drove, "You know, we're very lucky to be staying here. Uncle Thomas and Aunt Jane haven't even had a chance to come and visit since they bought it last month."

"Imagine buying a lighthouse. That's so cool!" exclaimed Emma.

"Yes, I think so, too," answered Mrs. Jones, joining the conversation before turning to look in the back seat. "What do you think boys? Are you awake back there?"

"Yes Mom, I'm awake!" Jack giggled, "I'm starting to feel hungry though..."

"Me too, Mrs. Jones!" added Albert.

"I guess it is getting close to lunch time. How about we drop off our things at the lighthouse, meet the caretaker to get the keys, and then we can head into the village for something to eat?"

Mr. Jones slowed the car as they approached a somewhat rickety-looking wooden bridge.

"It looks like this old bridge has seen better days," he said as he steadily drove across it.

"I think Uncle Thomas and Aunt Jane will need to fix this, it feels very wobbly," said Jack.

After crossing the bridge, it was only a short distance to the base of the lighthouse.

As they approached, they saw an older man standing beside a pickup truck. He waved to them as they pulled to a stop next to him.

Everyone in the car waved back as they flung the doors open and bounded out, excited to stretch their legs and move around after being in the car for so long.

"Welcome to Point Danger Lighthouse! I'm Harry, the caretaker here, and you must be Mr. and Mrs. Jones," the older man said as they exchanged handshakes.

"It's very nice to meet you, Harry! I'm Theodore – but please call me Teddy. And this is my wife, Penelope."

"Please, call me Penny," said Mrs. Jones with a warm smile.

Mr. Jones pointed in the direction of the children.

"It's sure been a long car ride for them – they'll be over in a minute to say hello. We are really looking forward to staying here and exploring this beautiful area," Mr. Jones smiled, watching the children run around in the new surroundings.

He continued, "Penny's sister and her husband are the proud new owners of this place, and when they heard we had a seminar nearby they insisted we stay here."

Harry nodded, "It's nice to meet you both. I remember Thomas and Jane, a very nice couple. It was only brief, but I was fortunate to have met them before they bought the property. However," Harry hesitated, "...if you are planning to stay here I feel it only fair to give you the same warning I gave to them."

Harry's face turned quite serious as he leaned closer and continued in a whisper, "Strange things happen around here. Things that can't be explained."

Just then, Jack, Emma and Albert came running over to their parents.

Harry saw them coming and quickly looked back at Mr. and Mrs. Jones, "Probably best not to say anything more now... I wouldn't want to frighten the young ones..."

Jack reached the three grown-ups first and held out his hand to Harry, "Hello, I'm Jack... Jack Jones."

Harry shook Jack's hand, "I'm Harry. Pleased to meet you, Jack."

"This is my sister, Emma, and my best friend, Albert."

Harry looked at the three children, pausing for a moment, considering how much he should say. "I think you will have a fine enough time here. There are plenty of areas to explore, and a lot of fun to be had, but do stick together... and be careful."

Before anyone could read too deeply into his warning, Harry offered to take everyone on a quick tour to show them all around. They were all very keen to learn more about Point Danger and its historic lighthouse.

"Things are a little rundown I'm afraid. The lighthouse hasn't been operational for over twenty years now. I keep things tidy and fix what needs fixing, when funds permit that is, but there are a few leaks here and there," explained Harry.

Mr. and Mrs. Jones nodded.

"Do you know what your sister and her husband plan to do with the place?" Harry asked curiously as they began walking.

"From what my sister tells me, they had been up here on vacation many times over the years and when they heard the lighthouse was for sale they just couldn't help themselves!" replied Mrs. Jones, "They're planning to turn it into a guest house for people who come to visit the area."

"A guest house, you say? That will be interesting..." replied Harry with a nervous chuckle.

CHAPTER TWO

The lighthouse itself was five-stories tall and built of brick. It had been painted white with a large red stripe swirling around it and was set out towards the end of a rocky outcrop, with a stone terrace and protective railing wall built as a barrier against the sea.

Next to the lighthouse was a large main house, and close to that was a smaller cottage as well.

Both the house and cottage were built out of the same bricks as the lighthouse and were painted white to match, with red tiles on each roof.

On the other side of the lighthouse was a storage shed and workshop close to where the cars were parked.

As they walked together to the terrace area, Harry explained that the large house was the main lighthouse keeper's residence and the smaller cottage was for the assistant keeper. The storage shed and workshop, Harry told them, was where he kept his tools and did his work.

"Wow, that view is incredible!" Mrs. Jones exclaimed as they reached the terrace and looked out over the ocean.

"Yes, that it is," Harry agreed. "Just wait until you see it from the top of the tower!" he added, pointing up toward the top of the lighthouse.

Harry provided some more information about the lighthouse and the property.

"I'd recommend you stay in the main house, it is quite spacious and while not a swanky hotel by any means, you should find it clean and comfortable. There is firewood chopped and stacked on the porch at the rear entrance, it can still get cold here at night, this time of year. There's no food stocked, so, unless you brought some along, you may want to pick up some groceries in the village. No one has actually stayed here for a very long time and the locals all tend to stay away these days."

Harry looked around, thinking about what else to tell the group.

"It's actually an island, you know? That old bridge is the only link to the mainland, but there's plenty of space and places for the kids to run around and explore – there's even a pebbly beach on the south side."

Mr. Jones smiled, "Yes, I think we could spend a few weeks here and not be bored at all."

"True, I never seem to have time to feel bored, that's for certain!" Harry smiled warmly before turning serious again, "Look, this island and the lighthouse would be a wonderful place for you all to have a holiday if it wasn't for the strange things that go on here... just promise me you'll be careful."

"What sort of strange things?" Albert asked, a little concerned.

Harry peered at the ground, "I think I've said too much. Never mind the ramblings of this old man, I'm sure everything will be fine... just look out for each other is all I'm saying."

He paused for a few moments, then spoke again.

"I need to get going now, need to go two towns over this afternoon to pick up some materials to patch the shed roof again... more holes in it than a slice of swiss cheese," Harry chuckled at his own joke and everyone else smiled and giggled with him.

"I'll be back here tomorrow... this here is the master key, I hope you enjoy your visit."

With that, Harry handed a key on a keyring, shaped like a large buoy, to Mr. Jones

"You mean you don't stay here at the lighthouse?" Mrs. Jones asked.

"No way ma'am, I wouldn't dare... I'll see you tomorrow," said Harry as he waved and began walking back to his truck.

"What does he mean, Dad? Why does he seem so afraid?" Emma asked with a little worry in her voice.

"I'm not sure sweetheart, I'm sure it's nothing..." Mr. Jones replied, sensing he should change the topic. "How about we head into the village for some lunch now, then we can come back to get settled in and take a look around."

"Great idea! Race you to the car!" Jack said enthusiastically as he took off running, followed closely by Albert and Emma.

Mr. and Mrs. Jones looked at each other, slightly puzzled, "I wonder what all of that was about?" Mrs. Jones asked.

"I really don't know, he was behaving strangely, I agree," said Mr. Jones. They agreed to ask Aunt Jane when they next spoke.

Everyone piled back into the car and they drove the short distance along the scenic coast. The quiet seaside village was set around a small protected harbor that was dotted with fishing boats. It was a peaceful place where the locals appreciated a simple way of life, waving and stopping for a chat with one another as they went about their days.

The family made their way to one of the taverns and sat down in an empty booth by the front window. No sooner had they all settled into their seats, when a friendly waitress approached their table.

"Hello, I'm Nancy, welcome to The Rusty Anchor! Here are some menus, though I'd recommend the fish and chips, just caught this morning by one of our best local fishermen, fresh and delicious!"

Everyone agreed that sounded like an excellent choice, so they ordered five servings, one for each of them. Nancy smiled and went to the kitchen to tell the chef.

A few minutes later she returned to the table with cutlery, napkins, a jug of water and glasses.

"So, I don't think I've seen you all around here before. Are you visiting?"

"Yes, we are... my wife and I will be presenting a lecture at the university up the coast over the weekend and took the opportunity to bring the kids away with us for a few days," answered Mr. Jones.

"Ah... I see, that does sound like a good idea! Are you staying at one of the Inns in the village here?" asked Nancy.

"Actually, we're staying at the old lighthouse," said Mrs. Jones.

Nancy's face suddenly became quite serious and she sounded almost afraid when she spoke, "You don't mean the *Point Danger Lighthouse*, do you?"

Mrs. Jones paused for a moment and then calmly answered, "Yes, that's the place... why do you seem so concerned?"

"Oh my... there are a lot of strange things that happen there... they say that it's...haunted!"

CHAPTER THREE

Everyone at the table was quiet for a moment, all staring at Nancy, waiting for her to say more, but she didn't.

Jack spoke first, "What do you mean, *haunted*?" he asked curiously.

"What sort of *strange things*?" Albert added warily.

Nancy leaned in a little closer to the group and whispered, "I hear scary things happen up there. Harry, the caretaker, comes in here all the time with new stories. He talks about moaning and wailing noises. Footsteps when he's the only one there. Lights going on and off by themselves. He said he's even seen ghosts around the buildings!"

"Whoa!" gasped Jack, his eyes wide with wonder.

"And Harry's not the only one either... the caretaker before him used to say the same things happened when he was there," added Nancy.

She looked around quickly to make sure nobody else was listening, then she went on.

"Folks from the village here used to go there sometimes and sneak in – no mischief or anything, but they thought the caretakers were making it up, so they wanted to go and see for themselves. More than a few people all came back saying similar things happened to them. Once, a group of teenagers snuck in to spend the night. A storm whipped up and they came back all worked up in the middle of the night, dripping wet and talking about ghosts and noises. They were very scared... no one really wanted to go there after that."

"Really?" whispered Emma.

"Yes," Nancy nodded, "even Harry refuses to stay overnight there. When he first started working at the lighthouse he lived in the main house, but then too many things happened, and he didn't feel safe. The caretaker before him didn't see out the year."

Albert had a look of disbelief on his face "Um... is there somewhere else we can stay?"

"Could it be true, a *real* ghost at the lighthouse?" Emma asked.

"Actually, they say there could be more than one ghost," Nancy replied, a playful grin on her face.

Jack, thinking practically asked, "So who are these ghosts, and why are they there?"

"Well...," Nancy began, "the story goes back a few years now. I've lived here all my life and I remember when the lighthouse was still in operation. My grandfather was one of the lighthouse keepers and we'd visit him from time to time – I used to love exploring up there on the island!"

She paused for a moment, lost in childhood memories. Nancy smiled to herself before noticing the expectant faces at the table.

"One year, there was a very big storm. It was ferocious and lasted for several days. The keepers did their best to keep the light going but the relentless weather eventually flooded the utility shed and the light went out. Later that night, a cargo ship ran aground on the rocks and sank. All the crew were lost."

Her face was more serious now, "It was very sad. Not long after the accident, an automatic signal light was built up the coast and the Point Danger Lighthouse was taken out of service. They say the ghosts of the cargo ship crew haunt the lighthouse but can't leave because their ship sank."

Realizing how long she'd been talking, Nancy excused herself to check on their lunch order.

"Um, did Uncle Thomas or Aunt Jane mention anything about this, Dad?" asked Jack.

"Nothing at all, this really is quite strange...," replied Mr. Jones.

Nancy returned a few moments later carrying a large tray with all their meals. While they ate, everyone chatted about the stories they'd heard about the lighthouse.

Jack was interested in learning more, Emma was excited about the possibility of meeting a ghost, and Albert was concerned about the stories and what might happen to them if they stayed there.

Mr. and Mrs. Jones insisted that there must be some rational explanation for it all, and they all agreed to head back to the lighthouse to explore. And to make sure it would be safe to stay.

They reassured Albert that if the guest house was unsafe, they would relocate into town.

After everyone had finished their lunch, they thanked Nancy for the stories she had shared with them.

She felt a little embarrassed and apologized, hoping she hadn't scared anyone with her tales. She wished them a pleasant visit to the area and an enjoyable stay at the lighthouse.

Before heading back, Mr. and Mrs. Jones went to the local grocery store to stock up the kitchen cupboards for the weekend.

Jack, Emma and Albert took a walk around the village.

Quaint shops and restaurants lined the waterfront, while boats of varying sizes bobbed gently in the protected harbor as the afternoon sun shimmered on the water's surface.

As they looked around the town, they came across a small candy shop that was stacked floor-to-ceiling with large glass containers. They were filled with some of the most delicious looking candy, sweets and chocolate they had ever seen.

Mr. and Mrs. Jones agreed they could each fill a small bag as a special treat, so long as they did not eat it all at once.

After wandering around town, enjoying the sights and talking about ghostly possibilities, they decided it was time to leave.

After the short drive along the coast they arrived back at the lighthouse, this time with the added excitement of a mystery to solve!

They quickly put away the groceries, then the whole group set about exploring their new surroundings, and, of course, checking for any sign of ghosts.

It was now later in the afternoon, and it was agreed that the most important thing was to check the main house where they would be staying.

After all, Jack, Emma and Albert could explore the rest of the island the next day, while Mr. and Mrs. Jones attended their seminar.

Even though it was old and showing signs of neglect because it hadn't been lived in for so long, the main house was quite remarkable indeed. They could easily see why Aunt Jane and Uncle Thomas had wanted to save this property and why people would want to stay.

On the ground floor there was a large kitchen and breakfast room, dining room, library and lounge room. The second floor was where the bedrooms and bathrooms were, along with a nice den with a view toward the lighthouse.

Above that was a cramped attic that was accessed via an opening in the ceiling.

The home's location on the edge of the coast meant there were wonderful views of the sea and surrounding area from almost every window, as well as from the veranda.

The family spent some time looking around in each of the rooms and even popping their heads up into the attic.

They found quite a lot of dust and discovered many repairs and updates that would be needed at some point, but there were no signs of ghosts, nor anything to make them feel that staying in the house would be unsafe.

With everyone now feeling satisfied and comfortable that the house was a safe place to be, they set about getting ready for the evening.

Jack, Emma and Albert brought in some firewood and lit a fire in the kitchen area fireplace to help warm the house, while Mr. and Mrs. Jones cooked up a delicious big pot of spaghetti.

After dinner, everyone sat around the big table in the dining room and worked on putting together a puzzle they found in the library. It was of a lighthouse, though not the Point Danger Lighthouse.

There was some talk of ghosts around bedtime, but everyone settled quickly after a big day of traveling, and they all slept soundly through the night.

CHAPTER FOUR

The next morning, everyone woke feeling refreshed after having slept very well. The sound of waves crashing against the rocky shore and the chant of sea birds could be heard outside.

As Jack looked out the bedroom window, the warm glow of the rising sun lit up the cloudy sky with an eerie reddish tinge.

The smell of bacon wafting through the house drew Jack, Emma and Albert to the kitchen where Mr. and Mrs. Jones were preparing breakfast.

"Well, it's good to see everyone survived the night in the haunted house!" Mrs. Jones greeted them cheerfully as they sat down.

"Yeah, I slept like a log last night. I guess it could just be stories the locals make up to scare visitors!" said Albert.

"That's one possibility, Albert, though in my experience, a logical explanation can be found for most unusual events, providing you look hard enough, that is," said Mr. Jones as he served up the bacon, eggs and toast.

Albert thought for a moment, "I think you're right. But Harry seemed genuinely concerned yesterday. That makes me wonder if there's something more to it."

Jack smiled, "Good point. Well, we've got the whole day to investigate and see what else we can find!"

A knock on the kitchen door interrupted their conversation. It was the caretaker, Harry.

Mr. Jones opened the door and greeted him, "Good morning, Harry. Please come in."

"Thank-you, it's good to see you all this morning. Are you all alright?" Harry asked as he looked with concern, from person to person.

Mr. Jones laughed warmly and replied, "Yes, we're all fine... we had a great night's sleep here in the house and have been enjoying the area very much. Would you like some breakfast?"

Harry looked quite relieved, "Good... good... perhaps you won't have any trouble then. I've eaten but thank-you for the offer."

Harry pointed out the windows toward the sky.

"Do keep an eye out though, a red sky in the morning like this usually means trouble on the horizon. We're likely to get a storm later. I'm going to work quickly to patch-up the shed roof this morning and then head home before it hits... do take care – the storms can sometimes be quite fierce around here."

"Thanks, Harry. We'll be sure to batten down the hatches, as they say! Jack, Emma and Albert will be here today while Penny and I attend a seminar at the university. But we'll be back this evening."

"Understood, Mr. Jones. If you don't mind I'll get right to work then," said Harry as he headed toward the door.

"Absolutely! Good luck with the repairs," replied Mr. Jones as Harry left the kitchen and headed out to the shed.

"Wow, he really does seem worried, doesn't he?" observed Mrs. Jones.

"I agree, something seems to have spooked him alright. We really did a thorough check everywhere and couldn't find any sign of problems. Kids, are you comfortable being here today, or should we come up with another plan?" asked Mr. Jones, looking to Jack, Emma and Albert.

"We'll be fine Dad," said Jack, "I'm looking forward to climbing to the top of the lighthouse today, then exploring around the island!"

Albert thought for a moment before replying, "I think we're OK to stay here. There are three of us, so we can look out for one another. And we've got Jack's tablet, so we can call you if things get too...weird."

"If there is a ghost... or ghosts, I just hope they're friendly. I'd love to meet one!" Emma giggled.

"Hey, as long as there aren't any snakes, I think we can handle it!" Jack laughed back. He was certainly a brave kid, but when it came to snakes, harmless or otherwise, Jack preferred to keep his distance.

Shortly after breakfast, Jack, Emma and Albert were waving good-bye to Mr. and Mrs. Jones as they headed off down the driveway.

Once the car was out of sight Jack turned to Emma and Albert, "Race you to the lighthouse!" he yelled excitedly as he took off, sprinting toward it.

Emma and Albert were quick to chase Jack, who had already gained a small lead. It wasn't that far to run but enough that they all found themselves huffing and puffing by the time they reached the base.

Jack used the master key to open the door.

Once inside, the trio found themselves in a round room. To their left were some tables and shelves with what looked to be old lighthouse supplies neatly arranged into stacks.

On their right was the beginning of a long, spiral staircase, snaking its way up the entire length of the lighthouse. As they walked toward the center of the room, they looked above them and could see right up to where the lamp was at the very top.

"It's a long way to the top... anyone up for another race?" joked Albert.

"Way ahead of you!" Jack replied, as he bolted over to the stairs and began making his way upward.

"Hey, JJ, no fair!" Emma complained as she ran over to try and catch up.

Albert wasn't far behind.

CHAPTER FIVE

The stairs wound their way around the inside of the tower, and small, evenly spaced windows dotted the walls along the way allowing light to enter. The narrow stairs meant the three climbed to the top in a single file.

"Wow, the lamp is huge!" Emma exclaimed as she reached the top platform.

"Yes, it would have shone a very bright light far out to sea," explained Albert.

"Over here! We can go outside," called Jack as he opened a hatch that led to a walkway around the outside of the top level.

From the top of the lighthouse the view in every direction was magnificent; they could see up and down the coast, including the local village, the whole island surrounding the lighthouse, and even the wobbly bridge that joined it to the mainland.

Most ominously though, out to sea were dark and heavy clouds quickly approaching.

"I don't like the look of those clouds," observed Albert.

"I agree... seems as though Harry was right about a storm coming," replied Jack.

"Harry! Harry!" Emma waved and called down to Harry who was up on a ladder by the shed.

Harry looked around for a few moments and eventually up to the top of the lighthouse, waving back when he saw them. "Hello, up there! I see you found the top. Amazing isn't it!" he yelled.

"Yes, it is. And you're right, there's a big storm coming!" Emma called back as she pointed to the heavy clouds gathering on the horizon.

From his vantage point on the ladder Harry looked out to sea and a frown fell over his face.

He looked back up to where Jack, Emma and Albert were and called out, "That's moving quickly, I'm going to pack up here. I'll have to mend this roof another day, and you should get inside the house!"

"Understood Harry, we're on our way down now," Jack called back.

Jack, Emma and Albert climbed back down the lighthouse stairs and headed inside the house.

Raindrops were starting to fall as they arrived at the kitchen door. Harry packed up his tools quickly then stopped in the kitchen to say good-bye. He made sure the children were fine and assured them that the house had withstood plenty of rough weather in the past. But he warned them to be careful if the storm turned out to be a big one.

Then he left.

The rain started quickly and fell hard, the heavy drops beating like stones against the windows while the wind howled all around the house, and waves thrashed over the terraced area by the sea.

Inside though, things were quite pleasant, the logs on the fire burned brightly, filling the library with heat and light while Jack, Emma and Albert played board games together.

The fun swiftly ended when suddenly, an eerie chill entered the room. Emma sensed the hair on her arms stand up and felt goosebumps all over.

"Do you feel that?" Emma asked sounding a little concerned.

"Yeah, Em, I do... it just got a lot cooler in here. Maybe there's a window open somewhere?" suggested Jack.

"I don't remember any windows being open... and why do you suppose it started just now?" Albert asked, also sounding worried.
"Alright, let's go and look around to make sure everything is okay," Jack said as he stood up.

Emma and Albert followed Jack out of the library, both feeling unsettled and looking around cautiously. As the three turned the corner into the hallway they heard noises coming from above them.

Thump... Thump... Thump...

Jack, Emma and Albert froze in place.

"Are they footsteps?" Albert whispered, warily.

"Hello, is anyone there?" Jack called out.

Everyone waited silently, without moving for a few moments, but no answer came. All around them the sounds of the storm continued, the rain pelting against the glass windows, the wind whooshing around the wall of the house. Then, the noise began again.

Thump... Thump... Thump...

"That definitely sounds like footsteps upstairs," said Albert, still in a whisper and with more concern than before.

"Who's up there? This isn't funny," said Jack, bravely.

Just then, all the lights that were turned on started flickering erratically before turning off completely.

Less light came in through the windows as the storm brought heavy, dark clouds that blocked most of the sunlight and caused the house to feel cold and gray.

"Alright, keep quiet and follow me to the kitchen. My tablet is there, and we can let Mom and Dad know what's going on," Jack whispered as he started heading in that direction.

Whooooooooo...Whoooooshhhhh...
Thump... Thump... Thump...

"What if Harry is right? What if this place really is haunted?" said Albert, looking around nervously.

"This must be what he was talking about. I don't think I want to meet this ghost anymore," Emma whispered, her voice trembling slightly but doing her best to be brave.

CHAPTER SIX

"*Ahhhhhh*! What's *that*?" Emma shrieked, pointing to the window as she, Jack and Albert entered the kitchen.

Jack and Albert looked over and saw something spooky glowing on the kitchen window. It appeared to move and shimmer as the raindrops ran down the glass. After a few seconds, the lights flickered back on and the spooky glow vanished.

"What *was* that, JJ? Where did it go? It was a ghost, wasn't it?" Emma's questions were coming as quickly as her heart was racing.

"I don't know what that was Em, but there's definitely *something* happening around here." Jack was feeling unsure now.

Strange occurrences continued to stack up and he was having trouble figuring out some sort of logical explanation for them all.

Jack went to the kitchen door and turned the handle.

"The door is locked, so no one could have come in here." There was a puzzled look on his face as he tried to make sense of the situation.

As they stood silently in the kitchen, trying to figure out what to do next, the noises from above began again.

Whoooooooo...Whooooshhhhhh...
Thump... Thump... Thump...

"That's definitely coming from upstairs, it sounds kind of like footsteps. But I don't know about the other sounds," said Albert, afraid of what might be up there.

The lights began to flicker again before going out once more.

The strange glowing figure appeared at the window again causing Emma to scream, *"It's back!"*

Outside, the rain continued to pour down heavily, the wind thrashed against the house in powerful gusts, then the sounds returned once more.

Whoooooooo...Whooooshhhhhh...
Thump... Thump... Thump...

"Let's go back to the library, follow me," said Jack, grabbing his tablet from the table before leading the way out of the kitchen and through the hallway.

They felt the chill in the air again as they made their way to the library just as the lights flickered back on.

Once they reached the library Jack closed the door, which somehow helped to make everyone feel a little safer. They tried to figure out what to do next.

Jack, Emma and Albert sat around the table in the library. The storm outside persisted, though it seemed to be easing slightly. Inside the house, the sounds continued to come and go.

Whooooooo...Thump... Thump... Thump...

The lights also continued to flicker on and off, and every now and then they felt a chill blow in from under the closed door which caused them to shiver.

"I'm a little scared," Emma admitted as she looked between Jack and Albert, then back to the library door as the noises continued upstairs.

Thump... Thump... Thump...

"I'm worried, too. It sounds like someone is walking around up there but how could they get in? And what about the lights... and that *thing* at the kitchen window," Albert said in a concerned voice, his mind racing.

Jack thought for a moment, then said, "I don't know the answers right now, my tablet doesn't have any signal either. Must be something to do with the storm I'd say."

"Or maybe it doesn't work properly with ghosts around, like the lights?" Albert offered.

Thump... Thump... Thump...

Jack looked up toward the ceiling. "If there really is someone up there, why do they just keep stomping around like that? I think we should go and investigate..."

Albert shot a worried look in Jack's direction, "Aren't we best to stay here where it's safer?"

Jack replied confidently, "I'm sure there must be a good explanation for this... and anyway, if there *is* something dangerous in the house, then waiting here and being scared won't help for long."

The lights flickered again as Jack stood up from the table. "Come on, let's go and figure this out, I'm sure this isn't really a ghost!"

Feeling inspired by Jack's bravery, Emma and Albert stood up, too. Jack opened the library door, led the way into the hallway and headed toward the stairs.

As they reached the bottom of the staircase the noises started again.

Whoooooooshhhh...Whooooooooo...
Thump... Thump... Thump...

The sound could be heard again as they were about to start up the stairs. It was followed by a rush of cool air that blew past them causing a shiver and stopping them in their tracks.

"*Ohhh*, maybe we shouldn't, JJ..." Emma whispered.

But Jack remained calm. "Come on, we'll be fine."

And step-by-step they slowly and cautiously made their way up the stairs. When they reached the second floor they paused for a few moments, listening for where they should go next. The lights flickered on and off a few times yet again, followed soon after by the noises and a cool breeze moving quickly through the hallway.

Whoooooooshhhh...Whoooooooo...
Thump... Thump... Thump...

Emma huddled a little closer to Jack who put his arm around his sister and tried to comfort her.

"It's alright, Em, I think those noises are coming from up in the attic. We should go up there... I don't think this is anything that's going to hurt us."

"How can you be so sure?" Albert asked, his voice trembling.

He remembered reading a book about lighthouses surrounded by spooky legends. And some of those stories ended in quite hairy outcomes.

"Well, I can't be... not yet anyway, but it sounds and feels a bit different from up here. Come on, let's go check out the attic," Jack replied, and led them down the hallway toward the attic hatch.

CHAPTER SEVEN

The attic could be accessed by an opening located in the ceiling at the end of the hallway. A ladder fixed to the wall provided a way up.

They reached the end of the hall and looked up into the opening. Suddenly, a cold gust of wind blew over Jack, Emma and Albert and the same sounds could be heard much more loudly.

Whoooooooshhhh... Whoooooooo...
Thump... Thump... Thump...

"It's definitely coming from up there," said Albert.

"Alright, let's go... follow me," said Jack as he began climbing the ladder.

When Jack reached the top of the ladder he waited by the opening to help the others up, first Emma and then Albert.

The floor creaked as they carefully climbed into the dusty, attic space. It was dark, and the roof was low, so they crouched down and crawled around looking for a light switch, or any sign that could provide an explanation for the strange things that had been happening.

"Hello, is anyone here?" Emma asked warily, but there was no reply.

The floor creaked again as they made their way deeper into the attic. Suddenly, a cold gust of wind burst past them, followed by the now familiar sounds...

Whoooooooshhhh...Whooooooooo...
Thump... Thump... Thump...

"Look, over there!" Albert gasped, pointing toward the far wall.

"What did you see, Albert?" Emma asked, looking in the same direction.

Albert began crawling to the other end of the attic, "There's some sort of opening over here, come on."

Jack and Emma followed Albert.

He found a light hanging from the ceiling and pulled the cord to switch it on.

When they reached the other end, Albert lifted a wooden flap that was built into the wall.

Suddenly, the wind gushed in with a *whoooooshhh* and a *whoooooo* as it whistled through the narrow opening.

They looked out to see the heavy clouds and rain falling over the ocean but nothing more.

"Looks like a window, or perhaps a vent for the attic," said Jack.

"Yes, and I think this explains at least *some* of what's going on around here," Albert replied as he let go of the flap and it fell closed.

Thump.

Albert lifted and dropped the flap again.

Thump.

Emma smiled, "Ha! Well I guess that solves the mysterious sound of footsteps... and the spooky noises."

Albert crouched down to look at the flap. "Look, there used to be a latch here to keep this closed, but it's broken."

"You're right. Nice spotting, Albert," Jack agreed, "Here, we can push this small shelf in front of it to keep it shut for now."

Jack and Albert shifted the bookshelf along the wall to cover the flap and keep it from blowing open.

Just as they finished moving it into place, the lights began flickering on and off again.

"But what about the lights turning on and off by themselves... and the ghost in the kitchen?" Emma wondered aloud.

"Hmmm, I think we'll find a simple explanation for those too, come on, let's go back down to the kitchen and see what we can find," replied Jack.

Jack, Emma and Albert made it to the kitchen without hearing any more thumping, footstep sounds or spooky whooshing noises. Feeling confident that they'd solved at least part of the mystery, they were now even more curious to find explanations for the rest of the strange occurrences.

The storm outside was easing and starting to calm down, though it hadn't quite passed over yet.

Shortly after the three had entered the kitchen, the lights flickered a few times, then went out once again.

"That ghost is back again!" Emma screeched, pointing to the window, though not sounding as frightened this time around.

"Have either of you noticed that it only seems to show up when the lights go out?" asked Jack.

"Interesting," Albert replied, and all three of them stepped closer to the window.

Emma peered out, "Look, there's a light on up there...in the top of the lighthouse!"

"That doesn't make sense, all the other lights have gone out," noted Albert.

Within minutes, the lights flickered back on in the kitchen, the ghostly figure by the window had disappeared, and the light at the top of the lighthouse had gone out.

"Hmmm, I think we need to go up to the top of the lighthouse and see what's going on.

Let's get our coats!" said Jack enthusiastically.

Jack zipped up his lucky jacket and Emma and Albert put on their warm rain coats and ventured outside. Dodging puddles, they quickly made their way across the gravel yard to the lighthouse.

All three huddled with their hoods on tight and hands in pockets as the cold rain fell and the wind blew against them. Once they reached the lighthouse the group quickly got inside out of the rain and made their way up the spiral staircase to the top, where they had seen the mysterious light.

It was rather dark inside the tower, but the crew managed with the low light that came in through the windows as they climbed.

When they reached the top, they couldn't find any lights turned on, so they kept hunting around.

They climbed through the hatch and found themselves on the outside walkway around the top level of the lighthouse.

When Emma looked down toward the main house she could see that there were lights on inside through the windows.

"Hmmm, maybe we need to wait for the lights to go off in the house again?" she suggested as she looked down from the lighthouse.

"Good idea, Em, we'll wait here for a bit and see what happens," Jack replied.

No sooner had Jack finished speaking that they heard a *click* from inside and a light was suddenly illuminated inside the lighthouse tower.

"Look! Inside the tower, up on the ceiling, there's a small light on now," said Emma as the others gathered around to look up at it.

She then looked back to the house and gasped.

"Guys, you have to come and see this. The lights are out in the main house again... and I can see the ghost!"

CHAPTER EIGHT

Jack and Albert joined Emma where she was standing on the outside walkway of the tower and could see what she saw.

A distorted beam of light was shining on the kitchen area of the house, including the window where they saw the ghost.

Jack turned to look back at the light in the roof, "Ah, I see what's happening – this light is shining through the lens and then onto the house."

Jack thought back to the science lesson where Mrs. Beaker demonstrated the different ways light can be bent and distorted through lenses of different shapes and sizes.

"It looks like the shape of the lens distorts the light and the raindrops running down the windows makes it shimmer, so it looks a little spooky when it reaches the house."

"Look! I guess because of the way the lens works, there are actually several ghosts, one on the shed, and another on the smaller house... this is all starting to make sense!" added Albert.

Emma waved her hand between the large lighthouse lens and the house, blocking the light and creating a large shadow on the side of the house, 'I just stopped a ghost!" she laughed.

Jack and Albert laughed with her.

Then, another *click* could be heard and the light in the tower turned off.

They looked back to the main house and saw the lights inside the windows flicker back on again.

"My guess would be that this is an emergency light inside the tower here. It must have a battery back-up and comes on when the power goes out," explained Jack.

"Yeah! So now I guess we need to figure out why the regular lights in the main house keep turning on and off," Albert replied thoughtfully.

"Hey JJ, remember when we had that storm at home and the lights went out? Dad had to fix something in the electrical box, perhaps it's something like that?"

"Good thinking Em! Now we just have to figure out where that is."

Albert walked further around the inside of the tower. "I think I know where to start... the power lines seem to go to Harry's shed over there," Albert directed Jack and Emma to the utility shed where Harry kept his tools and had been mending the roof earlier.

"Good spotting, Albert. Let's go!" Jack, Emma and Albert headed back down the winding staircase, out of the lighthouse and into the puddles, rain and wind once more.

They arrived at the utility shed and found the door was locked. Jack used the master key to open it, and in they went.

After finding the light switch and turning it on, the first thing they all noticed was the amount of water dripping in through the ceiling. Spooky sounds could be heard as the wind whistled over and through the damaged roof.

They scanned the shed and found a lot of old and dusty equipment, and a workbench area with tools. Some were organized, and others scattered around.

"I think I see the problem," Jack said as he started shifting boxes out of the way to reach the electric panel on the back wall. Water was leaking in through the roof and dripping onto the panel.

Before Jack could reach it, a spark flew out of it and the light in the shed flickered and turned off.

"Be careful Jack, that could be very dangerous," Albert warned.

"I think we need to find a way to keep the water from dripping onto that panel," said Emma.

As they started looking around for something to divert the water with, the lights flickered back on.

"That's better," said Jack, "let's look quickly before it goes out again."

After searching through the piles, Jack found a plastic crate lid. It worked very well as a temporary cover to shelter the electric box and direct the dripping water from the roof away from it. This would do until Harry could fix the roof properly.

"There's a bit of water damage in here... I'd say this has been happening for quite a while," Albert said as they looked around the shed.

"This is why Harry thinks the place is haunted... imagine the lights going on and off because of this old leaky roof? Then add the strange noises from the wind and the ghostly lights appearing at the same time the power goes off... it all makes perfect sense *now*!" said

Jack happily as they prepared to head back to the main house.

"I'm sure he's going to be very relieved when we explain it all to him!" Emma added with a smile.

"It also explains why those other people who snuck in here during that storm would have had such a scary experience. Can you imagine how much scarier this would have been if all of this was happening in the middle of the night?" chuckled Albert.

"I can't wait to tell Mom and Dad about this!" announced Emma.

"And Harry, too!" Jack added, grinning.

The storm had mostly passed, and it was late in the afternoon by the time Jack, Emma and Albert made their way back inside the main house again. After hanging up their coats Jack carefully placed a few new logs on the fire to warm up the house.

The three friends finished off their game in the library just as they heard Mr. and Mrs. Jones' car returning. Jack, Emma and Albert all raced to meet them at the kitchen door, excited to tell them all about their very eventful afternoon at the lighthouse.

During dinner, they eagerly shared the events of the day over a delicious meal of roasted vegetables and clam chowder with crusty bread that Mr. and Mrs. Jones had picked up at the local market on their way back from their seminar.

POINT "DANGER" LIGHTHOUSE

They commended Jack, Emma and Albert for keeping calm and working sensibly to solve all the strange occurrences they encountered.

After a very peaceful night of sleep, they all awoke to a glorious sunrise.

When Harry arrived to begin his day, Jack, Emma and Albert ran across the yard to meet him at the shed.

At first, Harry wasn't sure if he could believe their story or not, but after they visited all the areas around the property together, he was convinced.

He even felt a little embarrassed about jumping to such an unlikely conclusion without investigating further himself.

Uncle Thomas and Aunt Jane were also intrigued by the story and very grateful to Jack, Emma and Albert.

They joked that it may have been much more difficult to get people to stay at the guesthouse if it were haunted.

Or, perhaps it might have been an attraction – to stay in a haunted lighthouse!

The rest of the morning was spent exploring the lighthouse and the island. It was another sunny Spring day with a light breeze blowing gently across the deep blue sea.

When it was time to pack-up and head home, everyone agreed to stop by town for lunch at The Rusty Anchor and let Nancy know all about what had happened.

She couldn't help but giggle gleefully as Jack, Emma and Albert told her everything they'd discovered.

"Well, I guess that puts an end to all the rumors about the haunted lighthouse. But now there'll be a new local legend of the three brave children who chased the ghosts away!"

Everyone laughed.

THE END

TITLES IN THIS SERIES

COMING SOON

The Desert Quest   The Mysterious Light

Castle on the Cliff   The Ghost Ship

www.jackjonesclub.com

ABOUT THE AUTHOR

Zander Bingham was born and raised on a boat. It was captured by pirates when he was just 12-years-old. He, along with his family and crew, swam to a nearby island where Zander spent his days imagining swashbuckling adventures on the high seas.

Well, not exactly.

But Zander did love boating adventures as a kid. And he always dreamed of exploring deserted islands and being a real-life castaway. He grew up cruising around Australia, the USA and The Bahamas. He eventually captained his very own sail boat, living aboard and exploring the Adriatic Sea with his wife and two young sons.

His thirst for exploration, his witty sense of humor, and his new-found passion for writing stories to read to his boys at bedtime, led to the creation of Jack Jones; the confident, brave and curious boy adventurer who is always searching for his next escapade.